TOOT TOOT

To Ellen and Amelia,
who went over the mountain with me,
and to Amy, a true friend
P. R.

For Janice
M. C.

First published 2009 by Walker Books Ltd
87 Vauxhall Walk, London SE11 5HJ

This edition published 2011

2 4 6 8 10 9 7 5 3 1

Text © 2009 Phyllis Root
Illustrations © 2009 Matthew Cordell

The right of Phyllis Root and Matthew Cordell to be identified as author
and illustrator respectively of this work has been asserted by them in accordance
with the Copyright, Designs and Patents Act 1988

This book has been typeset in Usherwood Medium

Printed in China

British Library Cataloguing in Publication Data:
a catalogue record for this book is available from the British Library

ISBN 978-1-4063-3079-3

www.walker.co.uk

ZOOM!

Phyllis Root

illustrated by
Matthew Cordell

WALKER BOOKS
AND SUBSIDIARIES
LONDON • BOSTON • SYDNEY • AUCKLAND

POOR PIERRE! He lived all alone at the foot of a sky-high mountain, and ah, his heart, how it longed for a friend.

"Perhaps," said Pierre, "I could find a friend on the other side of the mountain."

So Pierre hopped into his little red car, and off he zoomed to find a friend.

Up and up the road he zoomed.
At every bend he honked his horn.

Toot! Toot! Zoom!
Toot! Toot! Zoom!

TOOT! TOOT! ZOOM!

TOOT!
TOOT!

"Where are you going so *toot-toot-zoom*?" bleated Goat in the middle of the road.

"Over the mountain to find a friend," said Pierre.

"I've always wanted to ride in a little red car," said Goat. "May I come, too, and help you find a friend?"

"That is exactly what my friend will ask, when I find a friend," said Pierre. "Hop in."

So Goat hopped in, and off they zoomed, Goat and Pierre, up and up the mountain.

Toot! Toot! Zoom!

"Where are you going so *toot-toot-zoom*?" baaed Sheep in the middle of the road.

"Over the mountain to find a friend," said Pierre.

"I've never been over the mountain," said Sheep. "May I come, too, and look for a friend?"

"Hop in," said Pierre.

So Sheep hopped in, and off they zoomed, Goat and Sheep and Pierre, over the mountain to find a friend.

"May I honk the horn?" asked Sheep.

"That is exactly what my friend will ask, when I find a friend!" cried Pierre.

Pierre let Sheep honk the horn.

Toot! Toot! Zoom!

Then Goat had a turn honking the horn.

Where are you going so *toot-toot-zoom*?" growled
Bear in the middle of the road.

"Over the mountain to find a friend," said Pierre.

"We're coming to help," said Goat and Sheep.

"A friend!" said Bear. "What a good thing to have.
May I come, too?"

"Hop in," said Pierre.

So Bear squeezed in, and off they zoomed,
Goat and Sheep and Bear and Pierre.

"Alas," cried Pierre, "my little car cannot make it over the mountain."

"Then we must push you!" growled Bear.

"That is exactly what my friend would do," said Pierre.

So Goat and Sheep and Bear all hopped out, and they pushed and they pushed the little red car …

to the very top of the mountain.

"Many thanks!" cried Pierre. "Hop in! Hop in!"

So Goat and Sheep and Bear hopped in, and off
they zoomed, down the other side of the mountain
to find Pierre a friend.

Toot! Toot! Zoom!

TOOT!
TOOT!
ZOOM!

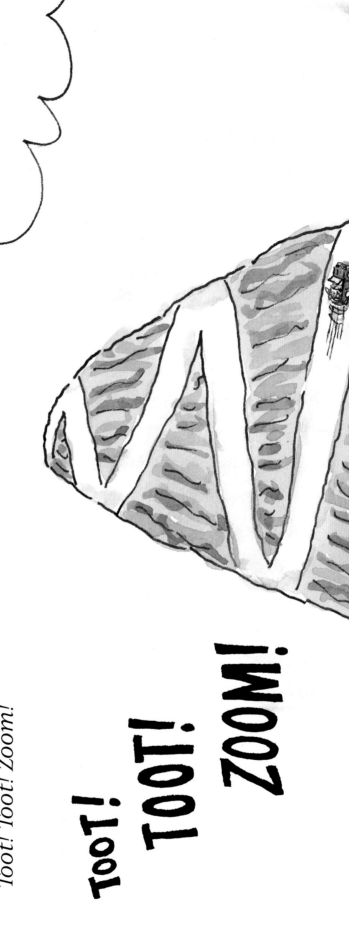

TOOT!
TOOT!

ZOOOOOM!

"Slow down!" screamed Goat and Sheep and Bear.

"No brakes!" cried Pierre.

"BLEAT!"

"BAAAAAH!"

"ROAOAOAR!"

"Is anyone hurt?" asked Pierre.

"Not I," bleated Goat.

"Not I," baaed Sheep.

"Not I," growled Bear.

"Not I," said Pierre.

But the little red car lay in pieces.

And alas for Pierre, no one lived on this side
of the mountain. What a long walk back
over the mountain it would be,
with no friends there waiting
to welcome Pierre.

"I shall have to stay here," sighed
Pierre, "but I did so hope
to find a friend."

"If you stay, I shall stay, too,"
bleated Goat.

"And I," baaed Sheep.

"And I," growled Bear.

"That is exactly what my friend would say!" cried Pierre.

"Then I must be your friend," bleated Goat.

"And I," baaed Sheep.

"And I," growled Bear.

"And I must be yours," said Pierre.

Not one friend but three – three friends for Pierre and three friends for Goat, and for Sheep, and for Bear.

And there they lived
on the other side of the mountain.

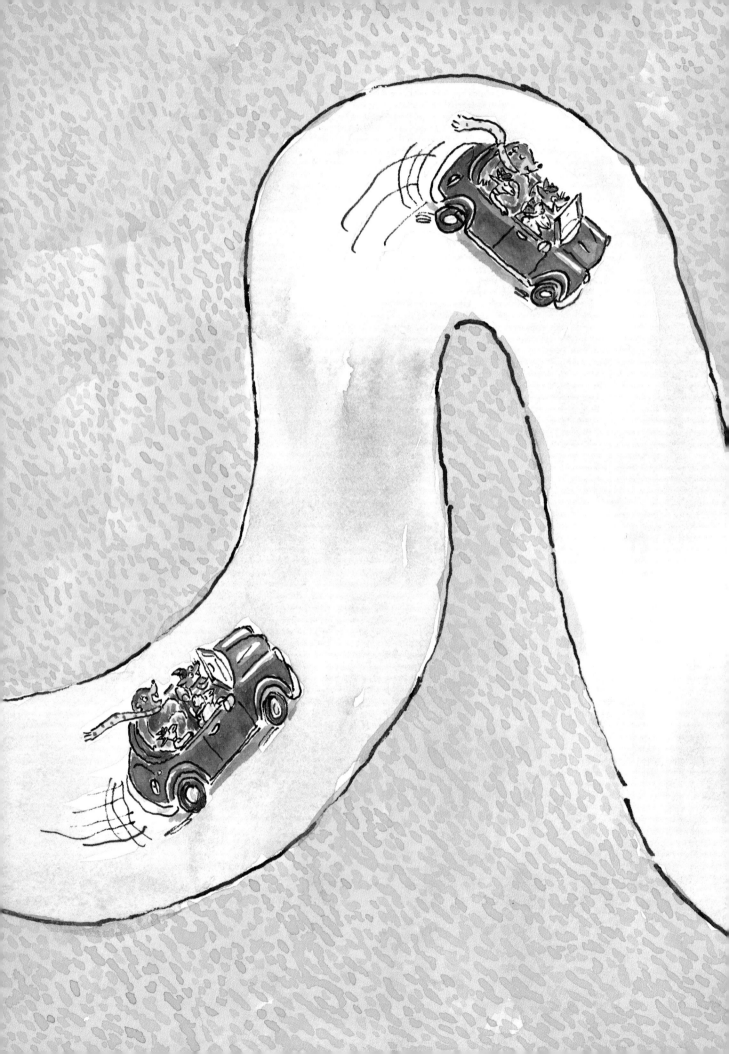

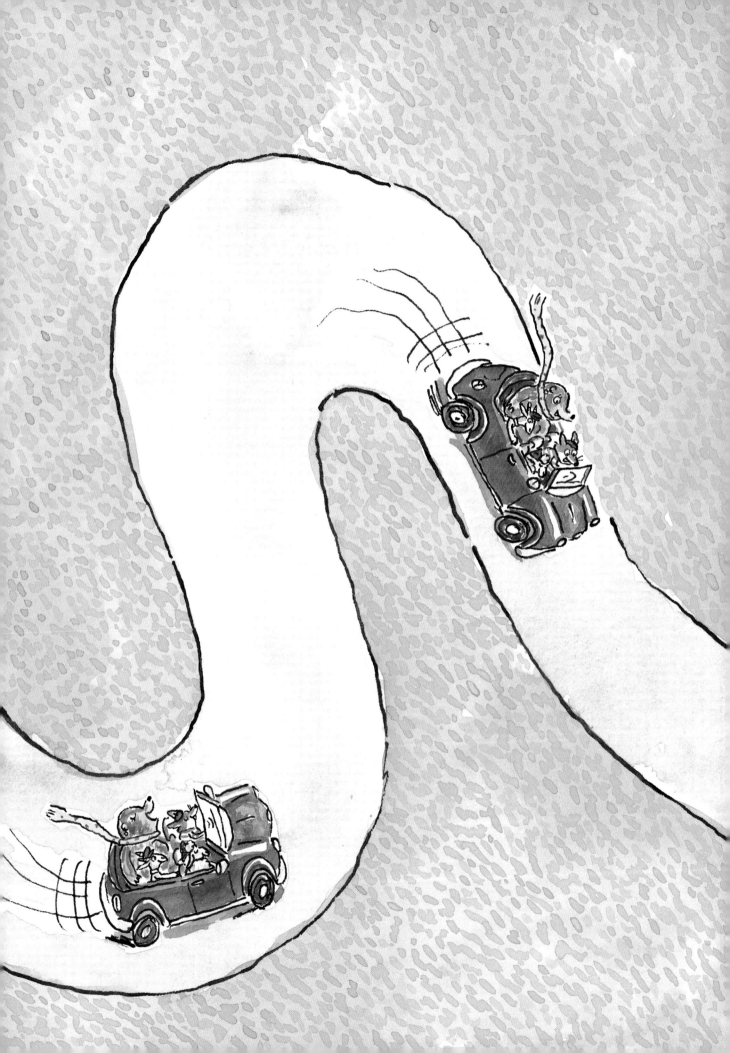

Phyllis Root is the author of more than thirty books for children, including the award-winning *One Duck Stuck*. About *Toot Toot Zoom!* she says, "The story arose out of driving through the mountains of Spain on single-lane roads, where people really do honk the horn at every hairpin bend to warn anyone coming in the other direction."

Matthew Cordell has illustrated several books for children. This is his first for Walker Books. About *Toot Toot Zoom!* he says, "I really felt like a perfect fit here. I grew up near the mountains of South Carolina, USA, a friend of mine once had a pet goat, and my first car was little, red, and ultimately went *ZUT!*"

www.walker.co.uk